Valerie Walder

HELEN BRADLEY

THE QUEEN
WHO CAME TO TEA

JONATHAN CAPE THIRTY BEDFORD SQUARE LONDON

by the same author

AND MISS CARTER WORE PINK
MISS CARTER CAME WITH US
"IN THE BEGINNING," SAID GREAT-AUNT JANE

To the Queen, with happy memories
of her great-grandmother

condition of sale
This book is sold subject to the condition that the Plates
therein, or any part of them, shall not, by way of trade or
otherwise, be made up for sale, or resold in any form other
than the form in which it is published.

First published 1978
Text and illustrations © 1978 by Helen Bradley

Jonathan Cape Ltd, 30 Bedford Square, London WC1

Bradley, Helen
   The queen who came to tea.
   1. Bradley, Helen
   I. Title
   759.2   ND497.B/

ISBN 0 224 01545 1

Printed in Great Britain by
W. S. Cowell Ltd, Butter Market, Ipswich

Miss Carter and Mr Taylor went off to the Town Hall, Manchester to see the King and Queen step from their carriage and enter. Miss Carter had a good view of the Queen standing against a background of trees and flowers.

THE BELLS RANG OUT MERRILY TO CELEBRATE THE NEW YEAR, AND THE YEAR WAS 1901. IT WAS to be a sad, confused year for all the ordinary people—the Queen was failing, they said, and men shook their heads. She had been Keeper of this Island of ours for so long that people couldn't understand what was to become of them if she wasn't there. Very little news came to our village of Lees so Grandma said, "Let us go to Oldham and see if we can find anything out. There should be some news." However Grandma, the Aunts and Mother pushing me in a pram didn't get as far as the Town because we met Alice Ann and her Mother who said they were sure the Queen had just died. Alice Ann was Aunt Mary's friend and her Father was our Policeman so Grandma said, "Oh dear, it must be so," and we all turned back and everyone called in at Grandma's house to talk things over. Miss Carter came wearing a much subdued Pink. (She always wore Pink, which colour, Aunt Mary said, didn't suit her.) "Do you think it's true?" was what everyone asked as the light of that January day faded. Then the Church Bell began to toll and everyone sat in silence listening, and a great sadness came over everyone. Grandpa went off to Huddersfield to buy a lot of black crêpe which was draped from bedroom windows all along the rows of houses and bows of it were tied to lamp-posts. All the ladies draped it round their hats and Mother stitched on broad bands of it across the front of Grandma's bonnet. Broad bands of it were also stitched round the men's tall hats and round the sleeves of their coats, and everyone brought out their mourning for it was a land in mourning and very quiet. "It is the End," they said. Everything had been the same for so long and now it was ended and the mourning and quietness lasted a year. Gradually our new King and Queen became part of our lives. The Queen especially did so much to make our lives happy and gay because she was a happy, cheerful person. She would stop to talk to people and she loved children and to her own young family she was known as "Motherdear".

We loved Great-Uncle Charles to visit us. He was an artist and lived near London and although he painted pictures he also loved other people's paintings and he and Father talked and talked about pictures. He also took Mother, the Aunts, Miss Carter, Mr Taylor, George and I to Manchester to visit lots of Picture Galleries. In one gallery he said, "Why, I do believe this is a painting of the Yellow Palace in Copenhagen. It looks just like an ordinary house in a row. Its front door stands open and there are children who've just dashed out and I'm sure the tall jolly girl in a blue dress could be our Princess Alexandra running to catch up with her elder brother." Then Miss Carter said she felt faint, so we had to leave. When we got home I told Grandma about seeing the picture of the Yellow Palace and the tall girl in the blue dress running after her rather austere elder brother. "Well," said Grandma, "it could have been the young Princess Alexandra with her young Brother and Sister, Willi and Dagmar. I believe that she and Dagmar shared a small room which was very plainly furnished and in that room the two sisters retrimmed their bonnets and made their own clothes because their father was not a wealthy Prince, and when Princess Alexandra fell in love with our young Prince Edward, Queen Victoria asked her to come and visit the Royal family, and when the young Princess stepped from the train, everyone who saw her was captivated by her friendliness and charm and do you know, she was wearing a bonnet she had made herself. When she became the wife of the Prince of Wales she had more money to spend and her good taste set a fashion in London society. Now she is our Queen and already she has done a great deal to influence the ordinary women." I looked at Aunt Frances, Aunt Mary and pretty Aunt Charlotte; even Mother seemed to have become much gayer, and our world had become an exciting place to live in.

I loved to listen to the Aunts and Mother when they met Miss Carter and Mrs Maitland with Emily in Spring Lane on our afternoon walks to the cemetery. They talked and talked about new hats and how they could make their hair look nicer and about the new sewing machines and shops opening in Oldham to sell materials and, said Miss Carter, there is a new pattern book by Weldons coming out, and happy were our days and our nights were filled with dreams of beautiful things. Mother let George and me off a lot of lessons so that we could hurry round to Grandma's to borrow the new sewing machine, but we still went our walks to the cemetery in the afternoons. The dressmaking lasted and we were never short of nice clothes to wear. I loved to listen to Aunt Frances plan Miss Carter's wedding outfit, because at that time Mr Taylor (the Bank Manager) was nearly out of mourning for his first wife, so he was beginning to look around for a second one. We all felt certain that he would choose Miss Carter, but she wasn't really a homely person so he remained very nice and attentive to her. "Perhaps," said Mother, "we haven't given him much time, but I feel sure there'll be a wedding soon."

In the year 1905 another wonderful thing happened, besides God coming to live in a shed up Springhead which was quite near to us. The King and Queen visited Manchester, and in the June of that year Miss Carter went to Manchester to look at the new summer dresses, and great was the excitement when she hurried along Spring Lane to meet us on our walk back from the cemetery. "Oh Jane, Mary, Frances, you never saw anything like Manchester. The King and Queen are coming on the 13th of July and stands and flagpoles and I don't know what are being erected, and bunting and fairy lights will decorate the streets. We must all go and see them," and Mother, Aunt Mary, Aunt Frances and Grandma stood in the middle of Spring Lane talking all together about their hats and dresses and what would be right to wear before the Queen. As the time approached everyone became anxious that the day should be warm and fine. Lots of times George and I pretended we wanted to see David Thomas's garden down Milking Green, but we really wanted to see if God was still on his shed because we thought the nearer we got to God, the easier it would be for us to call him. "Please God, let it be a nice day when the King and Queen come to Manchester. She thinks a lot about you and she's very good and beautiful." The weather did turn warm and fine, so just before the Great Day Grandma, Mother, the Aunts and Miss Carter went into Oldham to buy new hats. We always went to Mrs Bowers's hat shop in Union Street. She had good taste and always the latest fashion. We wrote to Uncle John, who lived in Manchester, asking him to find a good place for us to stand, and on the Great Day there was Uncle John with the landau and Prince ready to drive us to our places. We waited a long time and at last we heard cheering and knew that the procession was coming. "Oh dear, I can't see anything," and Uncle John looked down at me and said, "Come, I'll put you on my shoulders," and from that great height I could see everything. "They're coming, they're coming," I called, as the mounted Police came in sight. What beautiful horses they had! Then came the Queen's Royal Hussars and behind them the Royal Carriage and there was the King in a scarlet coat and the Queen in a lovely hat all made of flowers. She smiled and waved to me when she saw me, and I waved to her with both hands and I looked across at Wild's Toy Shop and there was God standing on the roof waving to her. What a lovely procession it was. There were more mounted Police and more carriages, but when the last carriage came in sight Uncle John said we'd better go and find Prince and our landau before all the crowds came. We soon got on our way to Uncle John's house and some dinner. The Aunts and Mother were tired and hungry and said how thankful they were for Uncle John's kindness to us. After dinner and a rest he drove us home. I don't think George and I remembered the drive back to Lees; we were so tired with the long exciting day that we slept and only awoke to find that tea was ready and Grandma saying that she was sure the Queen must be tired after such a long day. "Grandma, didn't you ask the Queen to call at your house for a cup of tea?" "Well, well," said Grandma, "I believe I did, so we'd better all get home in case she calls." "I'm sure she'll come, Grandma." Then George and I, tired out, went to bed.

The next morning I asked if I could go and see Grandma, and there was Grandma in her front garden tending her plants. "Oh Grandma, wasn't it a lovely day yesterday and we really did see the Queen. Did she come to tea?" "Now my dear," said Grandma, "you must ask Aunt Mary." The front door stood wide open letting in the summer sunshine. I ran through the hall, past the stairs and through

Queen Alexandra taking my little cup and saucer.

into the kitchen. I knew Aunt Mary would be there thinking about the food for the day. And there she was with the kitchen table covered with all sorts of nice things. The meat was already cooking in the big black oven and on the hearth was the bread crock already filled with rising dough. "Aunt Mary—it's muffins for tea—but didn't the Queen call in to see Grandma?" "She did," said Aunt Mary, "and she said, 'Aunt Mary, how do you make Yorkshire pudding? My husband, the King, is very fond of it, and somehow I can't get it light and crispy'." "Well ma'am," Aunt Mary had said, "whilst you drink your tea I'll show you how to make the batter. The children are coming to dinner tomorrow and it won't hurt to let it stand." Then Aunt Mary weighed out the flour and beat up the eggs and added the milk and beat it until it was like cream. Then she went to the pantry and brought out a cup with something in it. "What is that?" asked the Queen. "Ha," said Aunt Mary, "that is the secret of good Yorkshire puddings. I always put a little of the batter away each week and add it to the fresh batter—that makes it light." "Did the Queen say anything else, and did you look to see if she was wearing her crown?" "Well," said Aunt Mary, "I do believe she was, but it's very rude to stare at anyone, especially the Queen, but she did say that if we went to London she would be pleased to see us and show us the kitchens in Buckingham Palace, which was very nice of her."

After the Great Day the women began to think about their hair. So many had just straight hair and used to brush it right back and pin it in a bun, which made them look very plain. One day Miss Carter brought back from Manchester the new Iron Curling Tongs, great heavy things which had to be heated in the fire, so as Aunt Frances was going out with her young man Aunt Mary said she would try them on her. Oh, the excitement when those hot tongs were clamped on Aunt Frances's hair. "Oh!" cried Miss Carter. "Oh!" cried Mother. "Smoke's coming off it," and her hair actually sizzled and a little bit fell out. But when all the curls and waves were piled up on Aunt Frances's head she looked beautiful, and everyone felt that when John Smithies saw her he would be sure to propose. Later I heard Mother say to Aunt Mary that he must have proposed that night and she must have said, "No, John," because he never called for her again. Aunt Frances, it seemed, had made up her mind to marry James Alfred when his Mother would allow him, and she was content to wait.

About that time a great new adventure began for women. It was started in a small way in our village by a young woman called Annie Kenny. She used to carry a little placard around on Friday evenings which said "Votes for Women." Of course we all knew her, and the Aunts soon joined in. Father didn't know anything about Annie Kenny, so it was not until Aunt Mary took charge of the small band of suffragettes that Father found out, and only then because Aunt Mary got her name in the paper. She went to London, to the House of Commons, and called out in a loud voice, "Votes for Women" so often that a policeman had to take her out. Father was very cross about it, he said that women were making themselves look foolish. Men would see to it that they never got the vote. All sorts of things happened that Spring. Annie Kenny marched with her women, including the Aunts and Miss Carter, to the Town Hall to meet Winston Churchill, who was our M.P. Mother, George and I walked with them, but the crowds were so great Mother decided to turn back and go home through the Park. We saw the big railway warehouse on fire. What exciting times there were—so much so that Father thought he had better get all of us away to Blackpool again, but everyone said, "No, we want a change," and change we got. Grandpa had bought a house in the Isle of Man and thought the sail backwards and forwards would do us good. So we went on the paddle steamers the *King Orry* and the *Mona's Isle*. They made a great noise and took quite a long time. Then the two very new ships started, the *Ben-ma-Chree* from Liverpool and the *Viking* from Fleetwood. They were the very latest in comfort and we enjoyed seeing our dear Aunt Anne every time we arrived at Douglas. Mother, George and I and the Aunts stayed with her for a week or so, then we would move back to Blackpool. Aunt Mary would ask Mrs Maitland or Emily, "Has anything happened?" "No," they would say, "except we've had a nice

This is the hat Miss Carter bought when she was on holiday in the Isle of Man. It was made entirely of ruched pink ribbon and at the back was perched a beautiful bird.

day's outing to Lytham." Everybody was hoping that Miss Carter would have become engaged.

About the end of the year a motor car appeared in Oldham. Father said cars would never last, they could never surpass the horse as a form of transport, but Uncle John was quite taken with them and thought they had quite a future. "Never," said Father. "Just think of the great lorry-loads of cotton and goods a horse can pull. Why, that car cannot even get up a hill. I've seen men and boys pushing it up Manchester Street and the noise it makes is enough to frighten the poor horses." But for all the things Father said about motor cars to Uncle John that Sunday afternoon it was not long after that he came home early and called, "Jane, come and look at Eliza." Mother was cooking, but she went to look, and there in the road was a small dark-green motor car. Snow was gently falling on it, and as it hadn't a hood the two armchair seats at the front and back were beginning to get wet. "Well," said Mother, aghast, "can you drive it?" "Of course," said Father, looking big and important. "Anyone can drive a thing like this if they can drive a horse. Hurry up and get something to eat and we'll go for a run." Mother covered up the seats with all the umbrellas we had. We quickly ate our dinner and away we went. Fortunately we didn't come to a hill until we got well past County End and into Yorkshire, then when Eliza saw how steep it was climbing up Springhead she refused to go. There were lots of men walking home so they pushed us to the top. We were getting into moorland country and it was snowing and getting dark. Eliza didn't want to go any further so Father said, "Get out and help me turn her round," so Mother helped and Eliza stood looking down the hill and away we went. "Jane," called Father, "we're doing fifteen miles an hour." "Oh," groaned Mother, "do stop, we're running away." George and I were delighted, but as soon as Eliza got to the bottom of the hill and had to start going up again, she stopped and refused to chug even a little, so as we were near to Bonnie Warfe's farm Father walked up the lane and dear Bonnie took us home. Eliza was a dark-green Renault and she was second-hand when Father bought her; there were many times when we had to find a horse to get us home. "Surely," said Mother, "our dear Queen doesn't own such a stupid thing as a motor car. Horses are far more reliable."

Little by little Father began to understand Eliza, and as soon as the Spring weather came Father said we would go and see Grandpa at Blackpool, just for the weekend, but Mother feared the worst and packed enough food for the whole day. The roads in 1910 were all granite sets and Eliza's tyres were solid, so we were thankful to sit by the roadside and picnic. It was growing dusk when we came in sight of the Tower and Big Wheel but Eliza had had enough, she just sighed and stopped. The dusk went, and the darkness came, but through the quietness we heard the clip-clop of a horse. He was a nice horse and didn't try to kick Eliza, which some of them did, so in no time we arrived at Grandpa's, very tired, very dirty and very hungry. The next day at breakfast Grandpa said, in a very sad voice, "Well, we're done for. Income Tax is going up to a shilling in the pound." Everyone was very silent and sad. "Shan't we be able to have any food?" I asked Mother. "I don't know," she said. "We shall have to be very careful," and that evening paper-boys ran along the streets shouting, "The King is dying." Very quietly and sadly we waited for news. It came on the 6th of May, 1910; the King passed peacefully away. Poor Queen Alexandra, she would be alone in the house she loved at Sandringham and she walked alone through the fields full of the young green grass and daisies and buttercups. Soon she would have to leave it and pass it on to her son, who was now King. He in his turn would pass it on to his young family, so the sound of children's merry laughter would once again ring through the lanes and the fields. Goodbye, dear Alexandra, a much-loved Queen. A Queen who helped the women to take a look at themselves, to curl their hair and make nice clothes and in time, get the Vote.

The Queen is Dead, she said.
The Queen is Dead — the Queen
is Dead — they said.
The Queen is Dead, whispered they.
The day went quiet, sad and grey,
for the Queen is Dead.
And windows closed their eyes
slowly, quietly, for the Queen is Dead.
Grandmother sat with a tear on her cheek,
for the Queen is Dead,
slowly twisting crêpe on her bonnet,
for the Queen is Dead.
All the bells tolled, on and on,
for the Queen is Dead,
and men lost their talk on that day
that the Queen lay Dead.
In lamplight quietly we sat,
quietly, silently we sat thinking of her.
She who had guarded the soul of our land
is gone, and unguarded in sadness
*   England lay bare.*

I wrote this poem for my Grandmother when I was very young.

WHAT a strange sad day the 22nd of January, 1901 was. Although I was too young to know what happened on that day Mother, Grandma and my three Aunts (Aunt Mary, Aunt Frances and Aunt Charlotte) never forgot the stillness; then the bells began to toll from all the churches and chapels and everyone whispered, "She is dead, the Queen is dead." Even the day shed tears for a Queen who had been a Queen for so long, and on the day she was laid to rest the churches and chapels were filled with her sorrowing subjects. "This is the End," said Grandma. "What shall we do?" and it was the end, the end of an era. "And," said Grandma, "we now have a King, we must look to him. God save our King."

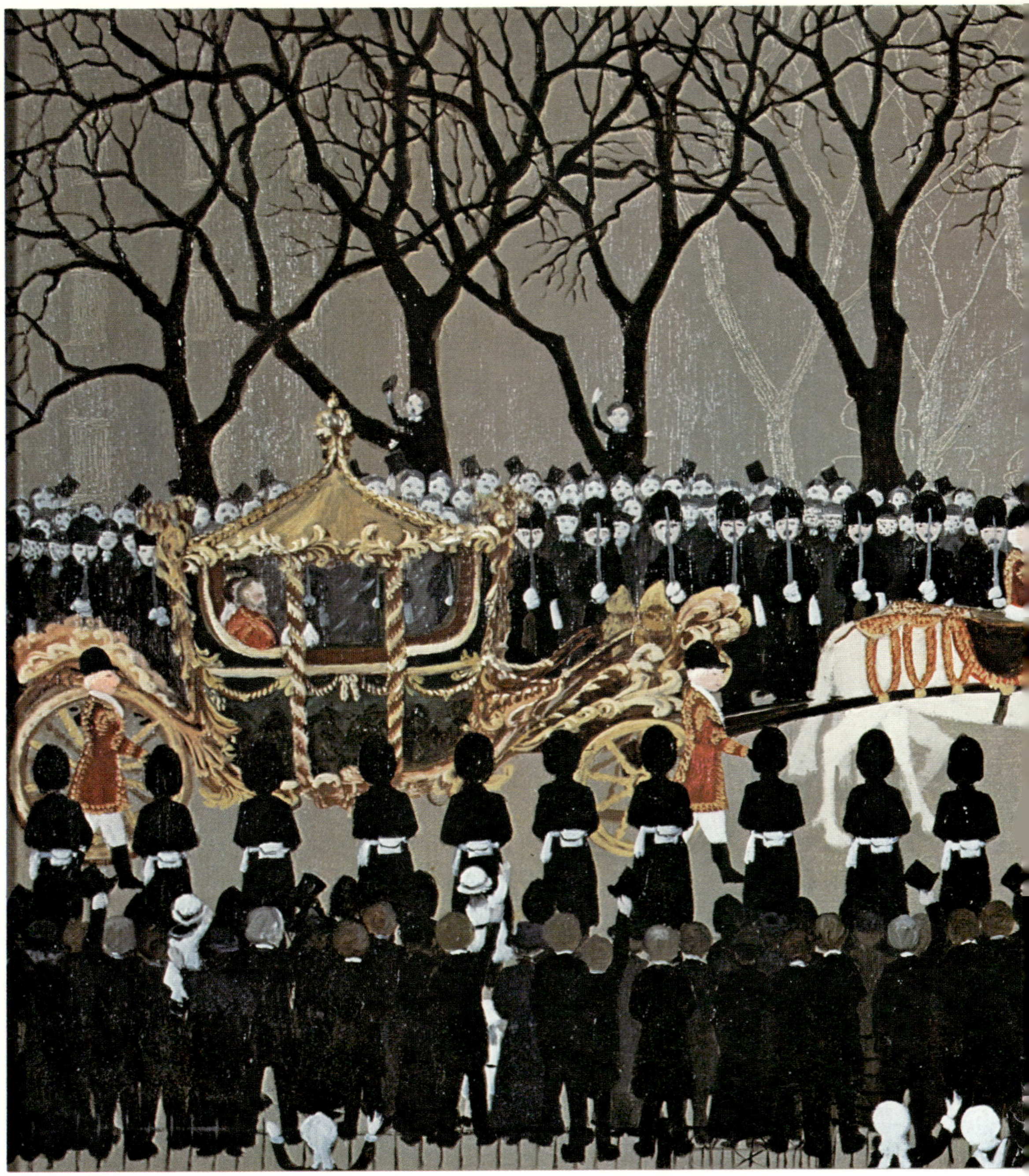

Now we had a new King and a very happy young Queen, and all the people who had felt so sad and lost began to brighten up, especially when a new paper called *The Queen* could be purchased from the book stalls in Manchester, and it was there that Miss Carter (who wore Pink) found a copy and hurried back with it for everyone to look at. Then towards the end of February Great-Uncle Charles wrote asking the Aunts and Miss Carter to come to London and stay with him in his hotel. They would all go and see the State Opening of Parliament. Everyone would still be in mourning because it was only a few weeks since Queen Victoria's death, so they went and saw the King and Queen drive down the Mall. Our new Queen looked beautiful, they told Mother when they got back home. She wore a black dress trimmed with diamonds, and her hair was all little curls — how had she managed it? And they looked at one another — and wondered!

GREAT-UNCLE Charles, Grandpa's youngest brother, was an artist and was great fun. Although he lived near London he spent much time in Paris. He talked and talked about pictures when he came to stay with us and he took Mother, the Aunts, George and me (also the dogs Gyp and Barney) and Miss Carter (who wore Pink) and today, Mr Taylor (the Bank Manager) to Manchester to visit Art Galleries. Great-Uncle Charles wasn't keen on taking Miss Carter, but as she always went everywhere with us, he couldn't really leave her out. As soon as we got into a Gallery and Great-Uncle Charles was telling us about pictures, she always began, "Oh dear, I think I'm going to faint," so we had to take her out. One day he found a picture of a large yellow house, which he said looked just like the Yellow Palace in Copenhagen. "And look at the children that have just run out of the door. I'm sure that tall girl in blue could be our own Queen Alexandra when she was a girl. The boy and girl running behind her could be her brother Willi and the sister she loved, Dagmar. They had no front garden and the front door stood wide open so they could run in and out and play with other children."

IN MARCH we went to Blackpool to see how Grandpa was getting on, and when we got there it was much warmer and the sun was shining. The trees in the Enchanted Garden came into blossom. The trees were old and every year Grandpa said he would cut them down and plant some better ones, but we loved the wild cherries and the crab apples which showered their blossoms down on us like drifting snow. Always in March the frogs came to the pond and George and I had our jam jars ready tied with string, but Mother said she thought it was a bit early for the frogs to be in the pond, so, "Don't take your jam jars today," she said, but when we got to the pond there they were. "It's full of frogs," cried George, "and we've left our jam jars." "Never mind," said Mother, "we'll come again tomorrow."

WHEN we returned home from Blackpool Grandpa came back with us as far as Manchester. He always said that he loved Manchester so whilst Grandpa was staying with Uncle John, Father took us down for the weekend. Mother, the Aunts, Miss Carter (who wore Pink) and Mr Taylor (the Bank Manager) and George and I, we all loved Manchester and it was exciting especially when Grandpa said, "What about taking the Ladies to see the shops? Prince could do with a good run," so out came the landau and Prince, Mother and the Aunts dressed themselves in their best muslins, and away we went. Grandpa's last instruction to Father was, "Now Frederick, don't forget to tie Prince to a lamp-post in Brown Street and give a boy a penny to look after him."

A FEW weeks after our day in Manchester Miss Carter went off to her special shop in Manchester to buy a dress, and when she got there she was astonished to see workmen everywhere erecting white poles and goodness knows what, so she asked a workman, "Why the fuss?" "The King and Queen are coming to Manchester, Miss," so she dashed home to find Mother and the Aunts, and how excited they were. "We must certainly go and see Their Majesties." Would their old muslins do or ought they to buy new ones? They decided the dresses would do, but they ought to have new hats so we all went to Mrs Bowers's Hat Shop. The new spring hats were lovely and such a change from the plain straw sailors with stiff straight brims and to keep them on women had to fasten them to their hair with long hat-pins. Mother, the Aunts and Miss Carter walked home carrying their new hats delightedly.

THE Great Day had arrived. Mother got us ready early and whilst waiting for Grandma and the Aunts, also Miss Carter (who wore Pink) and Mr Taylor (the Bank Manager), Mother made a hamper of dainty sandwiches and little cakes. Father came round with our little wagonette with Fanny — even dear Fanny was wearing her best hat. We drove to Manchester to meet Uncle John, then Father took Fanny back and left us with Uncle John, who took us along the route to see all the bunting and flags. People were filling the streets, the little girls in their white frocks and everyone in their best clothes, and down by the Cathedral there was the River Irwell with its steamer decorated with flags sailing up to Salford. The Police were beginning to clear the streets, so we went back along Long Millgate and saw the little Market. Then Uncle John drove us back and, as it was time to take our places, we ate and enjoyed our sandwiches and the day was 13th July, 1905.

To GEORGE and me it was a very long wait, but gradually all sorts of things came along the route. There were lots and lots of Policemen all going towards Victoria Station. There were lots of Policemen left behind who walked up and down keeping people in order. Children marched along with their teachers and filled the stands in front of the Infirmary and in front of us. Then there was a commotion a long way down Market Street, and, at last, we could hear a jingle of horses. "They're coming, they're coming, the Queen is coming," and now they came in sight. "Oh, I can't see them," I cried. "Well, well," said Uncle John, "come up on my shoulder," and what a glorious view I had. The Police came first riding their beautiful horses. There were a great many of them and behind them we could see the Queen's Hussars and then the four lovely greys and, "Oh it's the King and Queen, I can just see them."

As the King and Queen came near to us the children in the stands sang "God save the King". The Queen looked beautiful; she saw me perched on Uncle John's shoulder and smiled and waved. Then I looked up and saw God standing on the roof of Wild's Toy Shop and he was waving to the Queen. We knew he liked her and she thought a lot of him, and now there were more Hussars and Policemen. The other carriages came along carrying beautiful ladies and their gallant husbands, and as they passed Grandma said, "Wasn't it lovely and well worth waiting for?" and, "Dear me, it's one o'clock and time we had our dinner. Poor Queen, I'm sure she must be tired." "Grandma, ask her to come to tea, she can have it in my little cup and saucer." So Grandma said she would see, and then off we went with Uncle John to his house for dinner. We were hungry; afterwards he drove us back to Lees. By now, George and I were so tired we ate our tea half-asleep and soon we were in bed fast asleep.

WHEN I awoke the next morning I knew something delightful had happened the day before. Then I remembered Grandma and the Queen. I danced across to Grandma who was standing looking at her garden. "Grandma, wasn't it a lovely day yesterday, and did the Queen come to tea?" I asked her. "Now my dear, go and ask Aunt Mary." "Aunt Mary," I called, as I danced through to the kitchen. "Did the Queen come to tea?" "She did, and she said, 'Aunt Mary, can you tell me how to make Yorkshire pudding, my Husband is the King, and he's very fond of it', so I let her see me make the batter." "Did she have her tea in my little cup and saucer? I wish I could have been here to see her." "Well," said Aunt Mary, "she wouldn't have looked at you — you haven't Blue Blood." "Why isn't my blood blue and the Queen's is?" "The Queen was born a Princess and you are just a plain little girl," and whilst Aunt Mary was busy I found a needle and pricked my finger and a tiny drop of red blood came out — no, it wasn't blue so I must be just an ordinary little girl.

WHEN we all went to Manchester with Father, he always called on his customers down by the old Market. There were a few stalls, but what Grandma liked were the cheese shops. She loved cheese and would buy a half and sometimes a whole cheese after we'd sampled lots of them. We usually went on Tuesdays and not only did I like cheese, but I longed for a piece of pie out of a wonderful shop selling hams as well as pies. So on Mondays I watched the weather anxiously. I felt I ought to ask God to make sure it would be a fine day. Several times I would say, "Now God, please let it be fine tomorrow, we're going to Manchester, and please God let Father buy a piece of pie from Gouldburn's shop," but God, alas, must not have heard me because Father never bought any pie. One day the Tar Engine was in the street, but when Mother saw it she said, "Put your hankies to your noses and cross over away from those children, they've all got the whooping cough, they're smelling the tar to do them good."

AFTER we'd all seen the Queen, a new magazine came to be sold. The Queen, so it informed us, now wore the long straight sleeves—all the puckers and gathers had gone out of fashion. There was also an advertisement for the new face powder; it would be sent in a plain wrapper. Then the Aunts found what they wanted—the new curling tongs, so off Miss Carter went to Manchester to buy them. Aunt Frances was going out to tea with her new young man, so Aunt Mary said she would try them out on her. Aunt Mary heated the tongs and Mother read the instructions and Miss Carter made some tea. Then Aunt Mary clamped the tongs on Aunt Frances's hair and my, it sizzled and a bit fell out, but when it was curled and piled up like Queen Alexandra's she looked beautiful and when Mother saw her go with her young man, she said that she was sure he would propose to her, but Aunt Frances wouldn't accept, because I heard Mother say that she really liked James Alfred, our Chemist.

WHEN all the women began to take an interest in their looks and their clothes they also began to think they ought to have the Vote like the men, so a young woman who lived in Lees called Annie Kenny painted a sign with "Votes for Women" and began to hold meetings, and on Friday nights Mother took George and me to listen to her. But we soon got tired of listening although we enjoyed standing next to Big Joe, the Policeman who used to say "Be off" when men became troublesome. Of course Aunt Mary, Aunt Frances and Miss Carter joined the suffragettes. One day Winston Churchill, who was our Member of Parliament, came to Oldham, so Annie Kenny marshalled her ladies and marched them to the Town Hall. Mother, George and I and the dogs Gyp and Barney marched with them, but when Mother saw the crowds she said that we had better turn back. I felt sad at leaving Aunt Mary and Aunt Frances but Mother said that all those Policemen would look after them so we sadly turned away.

MOTHER said, "Don't worry, children, the Aunts will be all right," and as a special treat we could go the Park way home which took us over Gas Street railway bridge and we could stand and watch the trains going into Yorkshire. But when we got near there were a lot of people running. "Oh dear," said Mother when we got to the bridge. "The Railway Warehouse is on fire and we shall have to pass near to it," so George and I couldn't spend a happy half-hour watching trains. We had to hurry because the flames were going higher and higher even as we watched; we got past just before the firemen turned people back. The Aunts and Miss Carter arrived home for tea but they didn't think the meeting did much good, Winston Churchill wasn't very hopeful.

ON FRIDAYS Grandma, the Aunts, Mother, George and I, also Miss Carter and our dogs, Gyp and Barney, went into Oldham to the market. Miss Carter always bought her meat there instead of getting Joe Wroe, our butcher, to bring it for her. However, Mother, George and I walked on ahead to call at the Library. We also always looked at the pictures in the Art Gallery. There was a very large painting called *The Death of Cleopatra* and whilst we were in the Gallery a woman hurried past, went up to the picture and pushed her umbrella through the canvas shouting "Votes for Women." Mother told Aunt Mary and we all felt sad until we got to Lees Road and then there was a delicious smell. "It's Hot Pies, don't they smell good?" Everyone stopped and Grandma said, "How many shall we get? I think we'd better have a dozen. I can see Mr Taylor coming to meet us," so we carried home twelve delicious Hot Pies for our tea.

As TIME went on Annie Kenny joined up with the Pankhursts from Manchester and so Aunt Mary took charge of our small group in Lees. One morning Mother, George and I and Aunt Frances went to the station and there was Aunt Mary waiting for the London train. "Mary," cried Mother, "you're never going to London in that old coat? Why, I thought you'd given it away, it's bald and look at you in that old hat." "Never mind," said Aunt Mary, "I don't see wearing my nice clothes when you've to sit in those trains all that long time." Then the train came and she was away and we felt sad, but at teatime the next day she returned—safe and well. What a lot she had to tell. She even got her photograph in the newspaper because every time anyone got up to speak in the House of Commons she waved her arms and shouted, "Votes for Women" so loudly that in the end men shouted, "Take that Woman out," and two Policemen took her out saying, "Come along, Missus, you've got to go outside," so she came home.

"COME children, it's time to get up." That was Mother calling us. Already the sun was lighting up the streets and the people were already at work in the mills. We could hear the station horse clomping his big hooves outside our door as Father helped to load the big heavy trunks on to the station lorry. George and I were soon ready and eating our breakfast. Mother said, "Don't hurry, we've plenty of time," but we were too excited to take our time. Soon the cabs were standing at the door, and Grandma, the Aunts and Miss Carter, also Mr Taylor (the Bank Manager) were all coming with us to Blackpool and later to the Isle of Man. Father was in a bad temper, he always was when he saw all the luggage. He would stamp about saying, "Really Jane, you don't need to take the entire house away with us," but Mother was always calm, and answered, "Now Frederick, we've all got to have a change of clothes when we go away for so long." Just then Mr Taylor came and in no time all the bags and boxes were safely stowed away and we were off to the station.

WE ALWAYS felt anxious as we got near to Mumps Station. Everything seemed to take so long but Mr Taylor looked at his watch as we were passing Buckley and Procter's shop and said, "Plenty of time, we've a good half-hour to spare," and what a relief. Poor Mother, she'd been grumbled at by Father so much that she said she hadn't collected herself, and she fanned her face with her hanky, but the cabs were soon round the corner and at the station. The men came hurrying to take all our luggage. Father felt better now and told everyone to go to the Ladies Waiting Room. Mr Taylor said he and Father would look out for Willie Murgatroyd and Annie and their Mother. Then Father would call us, "Come in here quick, they're down there." Father didn't like travelling with Willie Murgatroyd because he ate all the time and was always sick. So into our two compartments we quickly settled ourselves, Aunt Mary carrying Martha and Nelson, our two cats, in their basket and away we went to a lovely holiday.

GRANDPA was at the station to meet us, and the next morning he said, "Would you all like to go for a sail to the Isle of Man? Your Aunt Anne is waiting for you, so Jane, what do you say?" Mother said she would love it, so everyone got ready quickly and we set off on the *Mona's Isle* from Fleetwood. She was a paddle steamer and made a terrific noise, but the sun shone and the sea and sky were blue. Aunt Anne was Father's young sister and had a lovely house close to the sea. What George and I liked best of all was to watch the three-masted schooner come in sight over the water. We could see all her sails billowing in the breeze and as she came nearer we watched the sailors fasten them up one by one so that she sailed into the harbour quickly and up to her unloading bay. Grandpa said she had sailed from Murmansk right up in the Arctic Circle and they'd sailed round the north of Norway and across to Scotland and right down to this little island bringing a huge supply of wood.

WE CAME back to Blackpool from the Isle of Man with Grandpa for our last week's holiday. Although it was late September the weather was still warm and sunny, so for our last night Mother said we could have a look at the sands and the sea and as we walked along we found some pierrots. They were quite good and sang such funny songs they made us laugh, but the tide was coming in so we had to go home. The next day we all set off for Lees and so that George and I should not be sad, Grandma said Big Bertha would be puffing along from Oldham bringing the Wakes to Lees, and the next day we heard the engine rattling down the hill to Lees Brook. Then she stopped and began to puff, puff up the hill to Lees. She was a huge traction engine. Tomorrow the roundabouts would be ready and we would all go to see them, and George and I would have a ride.

TOMORROW came and it was fine and sunny, but the roundabouts wouldn't be ready for us to go on until evening, so Grandma came and the Aunts and Miss Carter wearing her new hat and to pass the time we walked along Spring Lane and round the cemetery, then back to Grandma's to tea. Then we heard the music begin and Father took our hands and away we went to the Square. George, who loved engines, went straight to Big Bertha and Father lifted him up; one of the men took hold of him and let him look at all the working parts. George didn't want to come out, but he had his best white suit on and was beginning to get dirty. We went on the galloping horses and Mr Taylor won a coconut. Aunt Mary had made treacle toffee and crispy gingerbread for us. There was also a man selling Hokey Pokey. Soon they would be gone, but we knew Big Bertha would come again.

In the year 1909 Father came home with a motor car and in the first few weeks Eliza (as she was called) did nothing but stop, especially if she came to a hill. She made a big noise which frightened the horses and when she stopped Father got men and boys to push her to get her going. However, Father got more used to driving and said, "Let us go to Manchester and call on Uncle John." We got there without trouble and Uncle John was very envious. He wanted a motor car, so Father let him drive. On the way home Father said he might as well call in at Mr Wild's shop. We stopped unfortunately in the tram lines and when Father tried to get her to go, she wouldn't even make a noise, so Mr Wild very kindly said, "Frederick, thee can have th'orse," and with that he brought his horse and the boy fastened the traces to Eliza and off we went. Mother said she felt ashamed and pulled her veil down and put up her umbrella although it wasn't raining very hard.

WHEN the Summer came Father suggested we set off for Blackpool to see Grandpa. "Come along, just pack a few things for the weekend, it won't take us long to get there," but Mother knew different. She packed our picnic hamper full of food for dinner and tea without saying anything to Father. Even Father was glad of the stops we had to make to let Eliza cool down, and the picnics we had by the roadside were most welcome. The roads in the year 1909 were paved with granite sets and were very bumpy. However, the roads after Preston were sandy lanes and just when we could see Blackpool, not far from Grandpa's, Eliza stopped and just wouldn't go. It was growing dark and I wondered if we might have to stay there all night, then along the lane we saw a herd of cows coming. Mother didn't like cows so Father opened the gate and we watched them go by. Then Father asked the Farmer if he could lend him a horse. He did, and in no time we got to Grandpa's, very dirty, very tired and very hungry.

IN THE year 1910 Grandpa kept getting bronchitis, like the King, so Father thought we'd better go and stay with him for Christmas. It was a lovely holiday, Grandpa was feeling better and on Christmas morning when the sun shone on the crisp white snow, Grandpa said, "What about going to Jim's Farm and taking some crumbs for the birds and a carrot for Susie?" I loved Susie and popped some carrots in my pocket and away we went. The sun felt warm and we could hear the church bells ringing. Mother and the Aunts fed the birds whilst I called Susie. She came to the gate and munched the carrots and we wished her a Happy Christmas. Then home we went to a good Christmas Dinner, but, like the King, Grandpa died and we never went again to Blackpool for Christmas.

Poor Queen Alexandra. She would be lonely now, and would have to leave her beloved Sandringham. She had learned to love the country, it was so like her beloved Denmark. She loved the fields and the sea, her dogs and her horses. Her children were gone. George, her son, was now the King and he and his dear May would bring their young family to romp through the fields, and the house would ring again with children's laughter; so with a smile she thought, once I was Motherdear, but now I am Grandma, and I shall have more time for all those happy children.

Goodbye, dear Alexandra, you gave us so much – thank you.